for

Trixie

Naked Mole Rat Gets Dressed

Mo Willems

HYPERION BOOKS FOR CHILDREN/*New York*

An Imprint of Disney Book Group

There is so much to learn about the fascinating
little creatures known as naked mole rats.

But, for this story,
you only need to
know three things:

1. They are a little bit rat.

2. They are a little bit mole.

3. They are all naked.

Look!

Well, they *were*, with one exception. . . .

Wilbur,

   the naked mole rat

      who liked to get dressed.

Hello.

When the other naked mole rats saw him, they said:

"What are you doing?"

"Eeeeeewwwww!"

"Yuck!"

"I like clothes," replied Wilbur.
"When I get dressed I can be . . .

". . . fancy,

or funny,

or cool,

or I can just be an astronaut."

When the others heard that, they said:

"If you like clothes so much,
then why don't you open
a store or something?!"

"Yuck!"

"Eeeeewwww!"

(Naked mole rats can
be very sarcastic. . . .)

But Wilbur thought
that was a great idea.

The other naked
mole rats did not.

GRAND-PAH

They brought Wilbur to a
giant portrait of Grand-pah,
the oldest, greatest,
and most naked
naked mole rat ever.

"Look at that picture!" they demanded.

"Look at his heroic face!

"Look at his regal bearing!

"Look at his total lack of clothing!"

Grand-pah did look heroic.

Grand-pah did look regal.

But he would also look
heroic and regal in a casual
shirt and some summer slacks.

"Ugh!" said the other naked mole rats. "Don't you get it?"

DON'T WEAR CLOTHES!"

Why not?

asked Wilbur.

Something had to be done.

The naked mole rats marched right over to Grand-pah and told him all about Wilbur.

And then he asked, "Why not?"

Grand-pah was very wise.

He thought seriously about everything he had heard.

(Then he thought some more.)

Finally, he said in a heroic, regal voice:

"Gather the colony!
I shall make a
proclamation!"

When Wilbur heard about Grand-pah's proclamation,
he knew it was serious.

But he had no idea
what to wear.

In the end, Wilbur decided to play it safe.

Maybe not safe enough.

The others were so busy looking at Wilbur's socks
that no one noticed Grand-pah enter, until he
cleared his throat and proclaimed . . .

"Fellow naked mole rats! I had never worn clothes until I heard Wilbur's simple question: *Why not?*

"Why not, indeed? Do clothes hurt anyone? No. Are they fun? Well, they may not be for everyone, but this old naked mole rat wishes he had tried getting dressed earlier!"

(Then Grand-pah complimented Wilbur on his socks.)

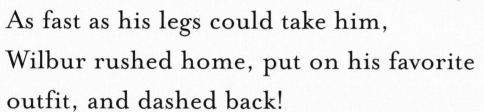

As fast as his legs could take him,
Wilbur rushed home, put on his favorite
outfit, and dashed back!

When he returned, Wilbur discovered he was not alone.

Much has been said about that day, but for this story, you only need to know three things:

1. Some of the mole rats were naked.

2. Some of the mole rats were clothed.

3. All of the mole rats had a great time.

No exceptions.

The End